A Pony to the Rescue

CHARMING PONIES

A Pony to the Rescue

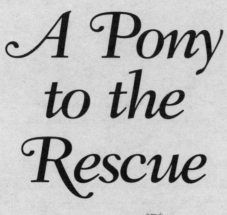

LOIS SZYMANSKI

 HarperFestival®

A Division of HarperCollins Publishers

To Dan, a constant source of inspiration.

Acknowledgments

During the course of researching the legend of the lost Silver Mine of Silver Run, Maryland, I was privileged to find several resources that aided me. One was a column written by Ruth Seitler for *The Carroll County Times*. The other, a remarkable book entitled *Ghosts and Legends of Carroll County*, written by Jesse Glass and published by the Carroll County Public Library, offered immeasurable assistance. Parts of this book are quoted within the pages of *A Pony to the Rescue*. To both sources I wish to offer a special thank you.

A Pony to the Rescue

one

Crackling logs spit sparks from the flames of the bonfire. Shannon sat on her sled, yanked off her snow-soaked mittens, and placed them on a rock near the fire to dry. The moon was bright, casting its light eerily over the group of friends. Some sat on sleds, some on logs, warming their feet as they took a break from an evening of sledding.

Shannon threaded two marshmallows onto a stick and thrust them into the fire. "Do you want one?" she asked Amanda, holding the bag out to her friend.

Amanda took a marshmallow from the plastic bag, then passed it down the line to Ashley, Sharece, and Larry. Larry was the hired hand here on Christmas Tree Farm. Shannon's dad paid him to help with the daily chores of tree farming, and Larry came to work each day after school. He would graduate from high school this year and be off to college. Shannon knew she would miss him when he was away.

With Christmas just around the corner, this was the farm's busiest season. But there was still time for play. Larry had stayed after work to build a fire and join them for a sledding party. As Shannon's marshmallows caught fire, the others slid their own white puffs onto sticks for roasting.

"Ugghh!" Amanda exclaimed as Shannon blew out her marshmallows. Amanda stared at the blackened blobs on the end of the stick, then watched as Shannon blew on them one more time, then popped them into her mouth.

"Yuck! How can you eat them like that?" Amanda pushed her dark hair under her hat and grinned at her friend, brown eyes flashing.

"I like them that way!"

"My sister's weird," Ashley said, and everyone laughed except Shannon, who made a face at her little sister.

Ten inches of snow had fallen over the past week, bringing excitement to the valley of Silver Run. All day long, the kids had packed a path down the hill with their sleds, across the dormant cornfield, down to the pond. Then, Mom had brought marshmallows and hot chocolate and Dad had lit lanterns to line the sledding path. The moon was so bright the lamps really weren't needed, though. Nighttime sledding parties were the best, Shannon decided.

Larry sat silently, stirring the fire with a stick. The swaying branches of nearby trees made shadows dance all around him.

"Tell us a story," someone cried.

Shannon nudged Larry. "Tell us a *ghost* story," she added softly.

Larry looked at Shannon, then back into the fire before he spoke. "Do you kids know the legend of the lost silver mine of Silver Run?"

Shannon looked at Amanda. She was shaking her head no.

"I don't know that story," Shannon said.

"Me, either," Ashley chimed in. "Tell it, Larry! Tell it!"

"Tell us the legend," Sharece agreed. "Is it scary?"

"I'll let you decide," Larry said mysteriously. Then he leaned in toward the fire again. His blond bangs hung over his eyebrows as he stared straight ahead in silence. He pushed back his cap and began.

"A long time ago, a German man called Ahrwud lived near here, with his beautiful daughter, Frieda. Now, Ahrwud was a silversmith, and a good one, too. The things he crafted from silver brought customers from far and wide. Everyone wanted to buy a trinket, designed and made by Ahrwud. But his neighbors wondered about him. Every time they came to visit, Ahrwud was sleeping soundly in his bed, and this would be the middle of the day! When did he find time to make the beautiful silver spoons and candlesticks, jewelry and other things, if he slept so much?"

"Maybe he worked in his sleep!" Ashley joked, cutting the tension of the group.

"Ssshh!" everyone said at once. "Let Larry finish!"

"Frieda was young, but she kept the cabin clean, cooked the meals, and did the laundry. Her father left the cabin every night and usually didn't return until just before dawn. Often the local Indians came for him or brought him home again.

"Then, on Frieda's thirteenth birthday, Ahrwud came home with a beautiful brooch, cut from the finest silver. 'Happy Birthday!' he said as he handed her the piece.

"Frieda looked at the jewelry in her hand. It was oval with a pattern of cubic shapes cut into it so that it sparkled in the light when she turned it this way or that. Right in the center was a perfectly formed rose. It was surely the prettiest thing she had ever owned. She threw her arms around her father's neck and thanked him, then pinned the brooch to her worn apron.

"By noon the next day, Frieda could not contain her curiosity. Every time she looked at the beautiful brooch she wondered where it had come from. She just had to know! How had her father made such a beautiful piece? When did he find the time? Frieda began to wonder if all the townspeople's stories were true. So when Ahrwud awoke, she pleaded and begged with him to take her along that night. Ahrwud could not stand to see his beloved daughter so upset, so finally he gave in.

'I will take you to see the place where I get my silver and work it, but you cannot know where it is, so I will have to blindfold you!'

"Frieda was surprised that her father would blindfold her, but she agreed to do as he said. After her eyes were covered, Ahrwud grasped her hand, held a lantern high, and led her down a trail through the forests and fields. As they walked, Ahrwud told her about the silver mine.

"'My Indian friends have allowed me to use their sacred silver mine,' he told Frieda. 'But I have promised them I would never tell anyone else about it. They say if anyone else finds the mine, it will disappear and I will be severely punished. So you must keep this to yourself, my darling Frieda.'

"Frieda nodded her head solemnly, feeling the pull of the blindfold as she did. A moment later, her father closed a heavy door and removed the cloth from her eyes. Frieda was astonished at what she saw. They were in a giant cave. Its walls sparkled where veins of silver had been exposed. Piles of silver stones were in each corner of the room. A strong oak table was set up on one side and on it were many trinkets, brooches, pins, rings, and even a few candlesticks, some of them not yet finished. As Frieda watched, her father set to work on a piece of silver.

"Just before daybreak, Ahrwud blindfolded his daughter and led her home again. He made her repeat her promise to keep the secret. But Frieda wasn't sure she could keep this to herself, so on the way home, she broke the branches of bushes and trees, leaving a trail she could follow should she decide to return. Her father hurried her home, too preoccupied to see or hear what she had done.

"All day long, while Ahrwud slept, Frieda tossed and turned on her cot. Sleep would not come. She was filled with the excitement of what she had seen. Surely it wouldn't hurt to tell just one friend. So Frieda rose from her bed, bundled up, and hurried to visit with her friend Nina.

"It wasn't long before Nina and Frieda were following the trail of broken branches. Nina just had to see it for herself."

Larry straightened his back and took a deep breath. He stirred the dying embers, then added a log to the pile.

"That's not the end, is it?" Ashley protested.

"No," Larry said with a half smile. "You didn't want the fire to go out, did you?"

"Hurry! Finish the story," Amanda said.

Larry smiled again and leaned forward. As the new log caught, flames began to shoot high again and a faraway look came into Larry's eyes. Shadows filtered across the young man's face as he continued.

"It would have been okay if the girls had just looked and left," Larry said. "But you know how women can be!"

"Larry!" the girls scolded. "Come on!"

"Well, it's true. They couldn't just look and leave. Those two girls had to gather up sacks full of pure silver and even some half-finished trinkets, and take them along when they left. Breaking promises was dangerous back then, and it was a sure sign of trouble to come."

"What happened?" Sharece asked.

"That night the Indians came to Ahrwud's house for a final time. They dragged him and Frieda to the cave, and they were never seen again. But that wasn't all. The mine vanished, too, never to be found." Larry paused. "Only Nina lived to tell the story."

There was silence around the fire. Shannon thought about the silver mine and wondered if it was still in the hills, buried somewhere.

"Is this a true story?" she asked.

"They say it is," Larry said. "It happened up there." He motioned toward the hills. "Up on Rattlesnake Hill. And people say you should never visit Rattlesnake Hill at night. They say a big German man with a wide-brimmed hat wanders the hills after dark with a lantern glowing bright. Many have seen the ghost of Silver Run."

"Has anyone ever looked for the mine?" Amanda asked.

"Yes. Many have searched. Two have died. It is said that three men must die before the mine is found again."

Amanda whistled under her breath. The sound floated eerily into the night. Shannon grabbed Amanda's hand and they stared up into the hills, toward Rattlesnake Hill. The fire was dying down again and everything seemed to have a weird glow. Silver streaks of moonlight shone through the tree-tops.

"Who wants to make another run down the hill?" Ashley asked. She stood up, grabbing the rope on her sled.

Shannon looked down the long winding sled path, barely lit by the lantern's glow. "Not me!" she said.

"Me, either," Amanda agreed.

"I'm going inside," Sharece said.

Larry kicked snow over the fire. "I'll pick up the

lanterns on the path," he said. "You kids hurry on in. Shannon's mom is probably waiting."

As the girls trudged up the slope toward the old farmhouse, Larry turned down the hill. Shannon looked back at him. He was staring up toward the hills and she thought she saw a smile play across his lips.

two

Moonlight cut a cool, white path across the living room's hardwood floorboards. Shannon rolled over on her back, just out of reach of the light, and stared through the gap in the curtains into the night. Beside her, Amanda lay on her side, curled in her sleeping bag like a contented cat. On the other side of the room, Ashley and Sharece cuddled in their own cocoon of warmth, built by piling sleeping bags and blankets around themselves in a circle to block out the drafts. Amanda whistled softly through her nose as she slept, and Ashley mumbled meaningless words in her sleep, but Shannon was wide awake.

Somewhere out there in the cold moonlit night there was a silver mine, sealed away in secrecy. Somewhere out there a ghost could be floating over the hills, calling out for a soul who could not rest. Shannon kicked at her blankets and rolled to one side as the thoughts swirled in her head. Suppose the mine was really there? Suppose it was a treasure chest full of silver and trinkets? And just suppose . . . she could find it?

"Hey, you sleepyheads . . . it's time to get up!"

Shannon opened her eyes and pulled a strand of blonde hair off of her face. The curtains were still parted, but where the moonlight had entered at night, sunlight now cascaded into the room, bright and intense, reflecting off the snow outside.

Amanda crawled out of her sleeping bag, rubbing her eyes, her hair a mass of tumbled black curls. "I can't believe it's already morning," she groaned.

"Me, either," Shannon agreed.

"Morning always comes too early when you have a sleep-over party," Mom sympathized. "But every cloud has a silver lining, and today Dad's making breakfast," she added.

Across the room, Ashley bolted upright in her blankets. "Pancakes!" she squealed. "Is Daddy making Polish rolled pancakes?"

"You guessed it," Mom said.

"Mmmm." Shannon sat up. "Rolled pancakes. My favorite."

"What are they?" Amanda asked.

Ashley got a silly look on her face. "They're old pancakes we roll up around leftovers," she teased.

"No, they aren't!" Shannon scolded. "They're thin, and as big as the whole pan," she explained. "You roll them up with cinnamon or jelly. They're delicious!"

"I'm up!" Sharece suddenly said, and the growling

of her stomach could be heard all the way across the big living room.

As they hurried to the bathroom to brush their hair and teeth, Shannon could hear Dad banging around in the kitchen and her stomach began to rumble, too. Soon, they were all sitting around the big oak farm table, spreading cinnamon or jelly onto the golden circles and rolling them up to eat.

"Dad?" Shannon said as she bit into her pancake. "Id dare weally a wost silver mine?" She swallowed the mouthful and looked up expectantly.

"Don't talk with your mouth full," Dad reprimanded. Then he smiled. "Where did you hear about that?"

"Larry told us last night," Ashley answered.

Dad chuckled. "That boy loves to tell that story! I guess he had the hairs standing up on the backs of your necks!"

"Dad!" Shannon said impatiently. "Is there really a mine?"

"Well, I've always heard there was. The story has been around for as long as I've been around. Every town has a reason for its name and Silver Run is no different. The silver mine makes sense to me."

"But no one has ever found it?"

"Nope!"

The girls ate silently for a few moments, thinking about the silver mine, then Shannon had an idea. "Let's ride the horse up to Rattlesnake Hill today. We'll see if we can find anything."

"It's too cold," Ashley said as she shoveled in another bite.

"Yeah, Shannon," Sharece agreed, "and you only have one pony. Who gets to ride?"

Shannon grinned sheepishly. She was disappointed. It had seemed like a great idea to her.

"I'll go," Amanda said.

Shannon reached under the table and squeezed her best friend's hand. "We can ride doubleback."

❋ ❋ ❋

Christa waited patiently while Shannon pulled the girth around her belly. Her nostrils snorted warm clouds of air when she breathed. Shannon buckled the girth tightly to make sure the saddle stayed in place. She rubbed the thick white fur on the pony's side. Christa's winter coat felt warmer than an electric blanket.

Amanda rubbed Christa's nose gently as she waited. "You know," she said, "Christa blends right in with the snow. She's a great horse to use for spying . . . like winter camouflage!"

"Yeah!" Shannon agreed. "But we really aren't spying. There's no one up there anymore."

Amanda laughed mysteriously. "How do you know?"

Shannon felt a chill go through her at the thought of the ghosts of Ahrwud and Frieda watching them, or even worse, angry Indians! She pulled Christa's reins over her head. "Do you want the front or back?" she asked her friend.

"The back. I always feel better when I can hold on to your waist."

Shannon climbed up on the fence and slid into the saddle. She grabbed Amanda's mittened hand and pulled her up behind.

"Promise you won't go fast," Amanda ordered. Her hands gripped Shannon's waist like a vise.

"I won't go fast," Shannon repeated. "But I don't know why you're still afraid when we ride. Christa is the safest horse on earth."

"Maybe she is," Amanda said, "but then again, maybe there's no such thing as a safe horse."

Shannon patted Christa's neck and shook her head in disappointment. "You hurt Christa's feelings! Now why would you say that?"

"I told you before that I fell off my cousin's horse when I was little! It was a long way down. Then he stepped on my hand and broke my finger!"

"I remember you told me that. But Christa's not a big horse. She's a pony. And even if you did fall off, she would *never* step on you! You've been around her enough to know that!"

Amanda gripped Shannon's waist even tighter. "I know . . . but don't go fast!"

Shannon shrugged. It was useless to pursue the discussion. Amanda would probably always be afraid when they rode. With a tug of the rein and a squeeze of the legs she guided her fuzzy, white pony through the gate and up the hill.

As they rode through rows of pine trees, Shannon breathed deeply, letting the pungent aroma fill her lungs. "I love that smell," she said.

"Me, too!" Amanda pulled a deep breath in through her nostrils. "You're so lucky to live on Christmas Tree Farm."

Just then a rabbit shot across the trail. Christa's head dropped down and she pulled to follow the little creature, but Shannon kept the pony's head up, forcing her to stay on course.

At the top of the hill, they turned left, following the edge of the pines. Silence surrounded them as they moved up and into a ravine filled with tall trees. They could see the shadow of Rattlesnake Hill just ahead.

Amanda leaned forward. "There's Kirkhoff Road." She whispered it, as if someone could hear.

Shannon nodded and urged Christa on, up the hill toward the face. She could see the outcropping of rocks surrounded by tall pines and a few maple trees and bushes. It sure seemed like the perfect place for a cave.

Amanda gripped Shannon's waist tightly. "Look!"

Shannon followed her friend's pointing finger and saw a large buzzard circling just above them. Something in the area must be dead, she thought. Suddenly she had a funny feeling that someone was watching them. She turned quickly, scanning the trees and rocks, but could see nothing but nature: snow, trees, rocks, and the dark blue sky above.

"What's wrong?" Amanda whispered.

"I don't know. I thought someone was here."

"I got the same feeling."

Together, they watched the bushes. Everything seemed still and quiet.

Beside a large boulder, Shannon dismounted and Amanda practically tumbled off with her. "Hey!" she squealed as she landed in the fluffy snow.

"Sorry."

They circled the boulder. Behind it was a big pile of shale and other rocks. Shannon watched as Amanda rubbed her hand along the boulder's crust, searching for an opening. Some parts were covered with snow, but others had been dusted clean by the wind. Amanda's hand stopped suddenly and retraced its movement over a section of the boulder.

"What is it?" Shannon asked.

"I'm not sure. It felt like it was raised up or something." They brushed the snow away from the rock but found that it was just a long ridge.

They were turning to go when Shannon saw a section of rock that was suspiciously wiped clean of snow. It was in a shady area, sheltered from the wind, yet it was clean! She hurried to examine the spot.

Sunlight nearly blinded her, reflecting off the snow and the silvery gray rocks. Then she saw it.

"Look!" she squealed excitedly.

Amanda looked, then gasped.

Shannon removed her gloves and ran her fingers over the indentations in the rock. Carved into it in jagged, uneven stick letters were three short words . . . "Ahrwud and Frieda."

three

The girls stared at the rock in amazement. The letters were not deep. It was as though they had been scratched into the rock with a sharp object. Shannon looked around. Had the carving been done recently? Or long ago? Snow *had* been wiped from the rock. That much was obvious. But there were no tracks in the snow. No sign that anyone had come and gone.

Amanda touched the rock lightly, running her fingers across the letters. "What do you think?" she asked.

"I don't know." Shannon wasn't sure why she was whispering, or why she still had that awful feeling that someone was watching them.

She pulled the gloves on again. "Let's get out of here," she whispered.

Christa's hooves clicked against the rocks where the snow had been blown clear. She picked her way down the hill and through the valley, toward home. Shannon and Amanda didn't talk for awhile. It was quiet in the hills, hauntingly quiet.

Shannon reached down and patted Christa's neck. She loved her pony. Something about having Christa with her made her feel braver.

Even if something back there was watching us, she thought, *I have Christa to keep me safe. No one can run as fast as my pony. Not even a ghost.*

But who carved that in the rock? she wondered. *Ahrwud and Frieda?* She could still see the words, even feel them under her fingertips, though she and Amanda were leaving the rocks and boulders far behind.

"Do you think the ghost of Ahrwud or Frieda carved their names?"

Amanda's voice echoing her own thoughts startled Shannon. She sat up straighter in the saddle and considered the question.

"I don't know," she finally answered, "but it looks too new to have been there a long time."

"Larry did tell the story right outside, in the open, where anyone could hear," Amanda said.

Shannon shivered. "I just don't know," she said again. "Maybe one of the people who searched for the mine earlier carved it."

"Yeah," Amanda agreed. "It could have been someone else."

"Suppose it was Ahrwud, though. Suppose it was his way of asking for help?"

"Larry didn't say anything about the carving in the rock. If it had been there for a long time, he would have told us."

Shannon rubbed Christa's neck. She was thinking of things they could do to find out more. "Let's go to the library," she suggested. "Maybe we can find out something about the legend there."

"That's a great idea!"

Shannon nudged Christa into a trot. "If we hurry, Mom can take us today, on her way into town to get groceries."

"Sssh!" The librarian gave Shannon and Amanda a stern look. They *had* been talking a little too loud, Shannon realized. They were sitting on the floor, leafing through books in the section on legends, looking for something—anything—about the legend of the lost silver mine. So far they hadn't found one single thing.

Amanda leaned close to Shannon and whispered, "I checked the computer. It said all the books on legends are in this section."

Shannon sighed with discouragement. Then she saw a pair of brown leather shoes connected to legs with stockings, and a pink, flowered skirt.

"Can I help you girls with something?" The librarian had lost her stern look. "You seem to be having trouble locating what you want."

Shannon stood up and brushed off her jeans. "Yes," she said. "We want to find something about the legend of the lost silver mine of Silver Run."

"I see," the librarian said. "Well, we don't have anything about local legends in the children's section. But we do have one book in Adult Reference. In fact, it was published by the library itself."

The librarian turned on her heel and hurried across the carpeted floor into the never-ending silence of the adult area. The girls trailed behind.

Just behind the information desk, the librarian reached down and pulled a book from a shelf. She handed it to the girls. "Remember to try and be a little quieter." She smiled before she walked away.

Shannon looked at the cover of the paperback

book in her hands. "Ghosts and Legends of Carroll County, Maryland," she read. "Compiled by Jesse Glass. Published by the Carroll County Library. Let's go to the study section," she whispered.

Amanda followed, through the rows of books and into the empty study section. They shared a chair at a desk in a cubicle. Shannon turned the pages until she saw a chapter titled "The Haunted Silver Mine."

"Read it out loud," Amanda whispered. "No one else is around."

"Everybody knows the town of Silver Run, located on the Gettysburg Pike about nine miles from Westminster," Shannon began.

As she read out loud the girls found that the story was just as Larry had told them. It had happened around 1783 and the Indians were the Susquehannocks.

"Larry wasn't just teasing us," Amanda said. "The story is a real one."

"Listen to this," Shannon said. "It's what happened when the Indians dragged Ahrwud and Frieda to the cave. 'The dance of death began,'" Shannon read. "'Faster and faster they circled Ahrwud and his daughter, making hideous chants and gyrations until the blood of Ahrwud and Frieda ran cold in their veins.'"

"What's gyrations mean?" Amanda asked.

"I don't know," Shannon said, "but I think it's how someone moves . . . like a dance."

"Oh. Read some more."

Shannon traced her spot with a finger, then continued. "'Suddenly the peaceful sleepers in Silver Run were awakened by two soul-freezing wails. The earth trembled and the winds whistled and howled. Over Rattlesnake Hill a fiery dragon with gaping jaws and terrible fangs was striking out in the sky.'"

She stopped reading.

"That's awful," Amanda said.

Shannon could feel a chill. It began at the base of her spine, crept up her neck and into her scalp. "I don't believe that part," she said.

"Me, either," Amanda said. "Remember what Mrs. Baker told us in class?" she said. "Legends are sometimes based on truth, but usually they get exaggerated. Sometimes they grow bigger and bigger until you don't know what's true and what's not."

Shannon nodded, closed the book, and stood up. "There's nothing about the carving in the rock," she said. "I guess we'll never know who put it there or when."

"Do you think we should keep looking for clues?" Amanda asked.

"Sure. I want to go up there again, tomorrow. Maybe we can find the entrance to the cave."

Amanda giggled. "Get real, Shannon," she said. "If grown-ups have already searched and they didn't find anything, what makes you think *we* can?"

"I don't know," Shannon said slowly, almost sadly. "But we are smaller. Maybe we can fit in between the cracks in the rocks and find places that grown-ups can't."

But even as she said it, she wasn't sure she was brave enough to go exploring in closed spaces. It was already scary enough up in the hills. Especially since she was sure that someone—or something—had been watching.

four

The next day was bitter cold. Shannon and Amanda stood at the bus stop, stamping their feet and rubbing their hands together.

Amanda pushed her soft mittens against her nose. "It's too cold to go up to Rattlesnake Hill after school," she said.

The wind cut through Shannon's jacket and she

hunched up, turning her back to it. "I know," she agreed.

At Charles Carroll Elementary School, students poured into the halls, gathering around lockers and chattering about the weekend snow. A path of slushy, wet, muddy footprints made a trail down the center of the hall, waiting for the janitor, who was mopping his way between the students.

It was the last week of school before winter vacation. In Shannon's fourth-grade class, Mrs. Baker tried to give a spelling lesson. Everyone fidgeted in their chairs, giggling and whispering until Mrs. Baker finally gave up. Sitting on a desk, she asked the children to tell her what they were planning to do with their days off.

Billy raised his hand, then stood up and told the class how he was going to Florida to see his grandparents. "It'll be warm there!" he bragged. "While you guys are freezing your noses off, I'll be swimming!"

"I'm not sure it will be warm enough for swimming," Mrs. Baker said, "even in Florida." Billy sat back down. Then she looked at Amanda. "How about you, Amanda?"

Shannon shot her friend a desperate look. *Please don't tell anyone*, she thought. But Amanda didn't look at Shannon.

"I'll be exploring," she said. Then she glanced at Shannon with a smile.

Shannon pushed her finger to her lips and shook her head. She put her finger down. "Don't tell," she mouthed. Amanda looked confused.

"And what will you be exploring?" Mrs. Baker asked.

"Oh . . ." Amanda stumbled over her words. "Just poking around in the garage. My mom is thinking about having a yard sale in the spring. There's a lot of neat junk out there."

"Well, that sounds like fun," Mrs. Baker said. Then she called on someone else.

Shannon sighed with relief. She bent over her

desk and wrote a note. *Amanda, that was a great answer! Let's keep this our secret. Come spend the night at my house on Friday and we'll make plans. Your friend, Shannon.*

She folded the note into a tiny square and passed it across the room to Amanda.

The rest of the week seemed to drag. It stayed cold and it got dark too soon. The two friends couldn't wait until the weekend. Then they would have two weeks of vacation for exploring!

On Friday night, Amanda came with her pillow, a suitcase, and a sleeping bag. "Mom said I can spend two nights," she announced.

"Neat-o!" Ashley shrieked. "We're going to have a great weekend!"

"We?" Shannon interrupted. "'We' doesn't include you. You aren't hanging around us. We have important things to do, *alone.*"

"No fair," Ashley whined. "I wish Sharece could come, too," she mumbled.

"Just remember," Mom said. "This is our busiest weekend for tree sales. You three will have to help out if it's busy."

"We know," Shannon said. "Don't worry about Amanda and me. We'll be too busy to get in anyone's way!"

At dinner, Dad talked about Christmas trees. "You know this is our last weekend for tree sales. Christmas is next Thursday," he reminded them, "and I'm going to need a little help from everyone." He looked at Shannon and Ashley. "Including you two! I'm glad you brought a friend," he added, with a twinkle in his eyes. "We'll put her to work, too!"

"It sounds like fun!" Amanda said. Shannon and Ashley groaned.

Dad drummed his fingers on the table. "Tomorrow morning, I want you to take that pony of yours up to the back pine field. Got a customer who tagged a tree up there last month. He was positive that was the one he wanted me to save for him.

Trouble is . . . I thought he wanted it cut. Now he tells me he wants it dug. Wants a live tree, he says."

"The ground is frozen solid!" Mom said with a frown. "How are you going to get a tree out this late in the season?"

"I already have that figured out, Martha," he said. "Larry took the tractor and tools up there yesterday. We dug around the tree and we were going to pull it out, but now the tractor won't start. Shannon, you're going to have to use that pony to pull it out. Larry will help you. We've got too many customers coming in tomorrow for me to go up there."

Shannon thought about all the times she had pulled cut Christmas trees down the hill with a rope and her pony. This would be a little harder, but it shouldn't take long at all, she figured.

"Okay, Dad," she said. "Amanda and I will meet Larry up there first thing in the morning."

Amanda's arms circled Shannon's waist. Christa carried them through the pines again. This time they were heading to the farthest tree field, the one that was just below Rattlesnake Hill. The sun was shining through the pines, flickering its light in checkered patterns on the ground. It was warmer than usual, and the wind had finally died down. Shannon lifted her face to the sun as they followed the broad trail.

Just ahead, Larry was waiting with his hand and chin resting on a shovel. "What took you two so long?"

"We had to saddle up." Shannon made a face.

"I've loosened the roots. Let's do this and get it over with. It's not going to be easy. The sun is making the snow all slushy. I hope that pony of yours can keep her footing."

"She can," Shannon boasted. "She can do almost anything!"

"We'll see about that." Larry grunted as he tied a rope to the trunk of the pine tree and straightened up. He handed the rope to Shannon. "Wrap that around the saddle horn tight now. When I say go, you make her pull. And don't let her get her legs tangled up in the rope."

Amanda swung her leg carefully over Christa's back and slid to the ground. "I'll just stand back here," she said, walking to the other side of the trail.

Larry got behind the tree, put both hands against the trunk, and pushed. "Go!" he shouted.

Shannon squeezed with her legs and Christa jumped forward. The rope went taut. Shannon continued to squeeze, urging the little horse forward. Christa strained hard, her legs kicking up snow and mud and slush in every direction. The tree began to inch out of the hole. Then suddenly it was up on the trail and moving along smoothly. Shannon pulled back on the reins.

"Whoa," she said. Then she patted the mare and smoothed her mane down gently. "Good job," she told her pony. "Good girl!"

A clump of dirt held the roots together at the base of the tree. Larry moved toward it with a roll of burlap in his hands. Shannon looked at him and laughed. Larry was spattered with mud from his head to his boots!

"What are you laughing at?" Larry demanded.

"You!" Shannon giggled, and soon Amanda joined in. Larry looked down at his blue jacket and work trousers. Then he burst out laughing, too. He looked like a leopard!

Shannon slid from the saddle as Larry pinned the end of the burlap into the root ball and began to wrap it around the roots of the tree. Around and around the cloth went, sealing the roots inside. Shannon helped by pushing a stray root into the burlap pocket.

Larry pulled a tiny penknife from his pocket and handed it to Amanda. "You cut the cloth," he told her. He held the two sides of burlap tight so that she could slice a path down the middle.

"A fine job!" Larry said.

Amanda closed the small, blue penknife carefully and handed it back to Larry.

"Now you tie it off, Shannon," Larry instructed.

Shannon had helped ball trees with her dad before. She knew just what to do. She quickly tied the string around the top of the burlap: two wraps, a knot, and then a bow.

Larry bent a wire basket around the bottom of the root ball to protect it. "Better get this tree on down to your dad," he said. "I'm going to work on the tractor awhile."

Shannon nodded and walked around to the back of the tree.

"Come on, Amanda," she said.

Amanda didn't look up. She was stooped down, examining the mud and dirt that had been pulled up with the tree roots. "Look!" she whispered excitedly. She picked something up from the slushy snow and mud, then rubbed it on her pants leg.

Amanda opened her hand. Shannon looked into the upturned palm and whistled. It was a brooch. A silver brooch.

five

Shannon glanced over to see where Larry was. She couldn't see his head. It was bent under the hood of the old tractor, where he was tinkering with parts, trying to fix it.

She took the brooch from Amanda's hand and examined it. It was dull from the dirt and mud, but it looked and felt like real silver. In the middle of the pin was an oval space, a place that could have once held a gem or precious stone. All around the edge, intricate designs were carved into the metal, and at the very top were three initials, F.A.S.

Shannon almost squealed, then caught herself in time. Whispering instead, so Larry wouldn't hear, she asked, "Do you think the F stands for Frieda?"

As Larry lifted his head from under the tractor and pulled a tiny part out, Amanda scooped the brooch from Shannon's hand and shoved it deep into her pocket. "I don't know," Amanda whispered back.

They stood and walked to Christa's side. "Give me a boost up," Shannon said loudly. She hoped her voice didn't sound strange.

Larry watched them climb aboard the mare. They began down the hill, with Christa pulling the tree slowly behind.

Shannon looked back over her shoulder. Larry wiped his greasy hands on an old rag he had pulled from his pocket, then lifted his hand to wave.

When they were out of earshot, Shannon giggled. "Do you think he knew?" she asked.

"I think he knew we were up to something."

"Do you know what I think?" Shannon asked. Amanda shrugged her shoulders and Shannon continued. "I think Larry's been planting *all* the clues. I think he's the one who scratched the words in the rock, then wiped away his tracks with a branch. After all he is the one who told us the story to begin with. He knew we would fall for it."

"It *is* funny that we never saw letters up there any other time when we were riding. It also seems pretty strange that we found the brooch in the dirt of a tree *he* just dug up!" Amanda was nodding quickly, getting more excited as she talked.

"Remember when we thought someone was watching us? Maybe that was Larry, too!" Shannon said.

"I bet it was!" Amanda exclaimed. "He's playing games with us."

"I'd like to get him back real good!" Shannon felt a smile spread over her face at the thought. "I think we should get even!"

Amanda hugged Shannon's waist hard. "Yeah," she

agreed. "We should think of a trick to play on him!"

As they rode through the trees, Shannon thought about how beautiful everything looked. The sun sparkled on the snow, creating shadows beside each tree. Christa's warm body helped to keep off the chill. Shannon ran her fingers lovingly through the mare's silvery mane. "I don't know how you could ever be scared of her," Shannon said to Amanda. Amanda didn't answer, but she did reach down to pat the furry pony.

As the girls got closer to home, Shannon could see the customers walking between the rows of pine trees, saws in hand. Every now and then one would stop to eye a particular tree, or kneel to saw one down. Excited voices floated up the hill.

A curl of smoke wafted from the wood-stove pipe in Dad's sale shack. Shannon could smell the hot apple cider and hot chocolate Mom kept on hand to warm the customers. Licking her lips, she squeezed her knees and urged Christa to hurry down the hill. She waved so her dad would see them and come for the tree.

That evening Shannon stood in her bedroom, rubbing the brooch between her thumb and forefingers. She laid it in her palm and smoothed a finger over the hole where a jewel had once rested. "I bet it used to be pretty," she said softly. "I wonder where Larry found it?"

"Maybe he bought it at a flea market," Amanda offered. She took the pin from Shannon. "We should wash it off."

Shannon followed her friend into the bathroom and watched while she rinsed it under cold tap water. She wanted to pin the brooch to her shirt. She wanted to touch it and make it hers. But Amanda had found it. The brooch should belong to her. Her eyes focused on the initials on the brooch.

"Earth to Shannon . . . Earth to Shannon! Hey, what are you thinking about? You're in a trance!"

"I was wondering about the initials. You don't think the letter F really does stand for Frieda, do you?"

Amanda's face clouded with thought. "No. I still think it's one of Larry's tricks."

Amanda wore the brooch to dinner. She had rubbed it until it was almost shiny, then pinned it on her green sweater. Shannon looked at it and wished again that she had found it. She watched Amanda touch it with her fingertips, then look down at it in admiration before sliding her chair in for dinner.

They were halfway through the meal before anyone noticed the brooch. Shannon's dad was in the middle of a sentence when her mom interrupted him. "Oh my goodness, Amanda! Where did you get that?"

Amanda's hand fluttered to the pin. "I found it today," she answered quickly.

"You found it!" Mom sounded excited. "Where? Where did you ever find that brooch?"

The look on Mom's face startled Shannon. Her mother's mouth dropped open and her fork clattered to the table. She jumped up and rushed over to examine the brooch.

Shannon was confused. What interest could her

mother possibly have in an old yard-sale brooch Larry had laid there for them to find? Maybe she thought it was real silver, Shannon told herself. Then she cleared her throat. "Amanda found it in the dirt," she explained, "beside the tree we helped Larry dig up today."

"It's Grandma's brooch!" Mom blurted out. She looked closer at the initials. "Frances Anne Schmitt," she said softly. "I never thought I'd find it again."

Amanda removed the pin slowly and handed it to Shannon's mom. "I guess it's yours," she said softly.

Mom took the pin gently. She rubbed a finger over it. "Thank you, Amanda," she said. "I thought this pin was lost forever."

During the rest of the meal, Mom bubbled over with enthusiasm. The conversation turned to talk of the old days when she was growing up on the farm.

"My mom sent me out to help plant seedlings with my pop. I was wearing the brooch that day. I was so proud of that pin! I couldn't believe Grandmother Schmitt had given it to me. Even though the stone was missing, I still loved it."

"You shouldn't have worn it to do chores," Shannon teased.

"I know that now," Mom said. "But I was just a little girl, then. We worked all day in the pine field, planting those seedlings. That night, I realized the brooch was missing. I searched everywhere for it, but I couldn't find it. I never did know what happened to Grandma's brooch . . . until now."

Mom gazed lovingly at the silver piece which she had already pinned on her collar. "Maybe I'll get a new stone set in it. Maybe a ruby. If it weren't for you, Amanda," she added, "it probably wouldn't have ever been found."

"I'll be dad gum!" Dad said. "What were the chances of you finding that old pin again?" He shook his head. "You must have planted it with that seedling."

Ashley giggled. "What were you trying to do, Mom? Grow more pins?"

Shannon and Amanda laughed, then Dad and Mom joined in.

When they were all laughed out, Dad shook his head again. "It's just incredible!"

Yes, Shannon thought. *It is incredible!* Then a shadow of a thought entered her head. If the pin was Mom's, it really had been a lost brooch. That meant Larry didn't put it there for Shannon and Amanda to find! And if Larry didn't do that, then maybe he didn't carve the rock either. And if he didn't carve the rock, then who, or what, did?

six

The next day it snowed, but not enough to cover the roads. In the morning, the customers came in droves. They laughed and kicked up the snow as they walked, obviously caught up in the Christmas spirit. One lady even lay down in the snow as Shannon and Amanda watched. Flapping her arms and legs wildly, she made a snow angel, then stood up to admire it before linking arms with her husband and trudging off to find a tree.

Shannon shook her head and laughed. "She acted just like us," she said.

"Except older," Amanda added.

This set Shannon off into a fit of giggles, picturing the older woman lying in the snow with her grown-up classmates, making a snow angel in the schoolyard.

Each customer was different. Some brought their own saws. Others borrowed saws from the sale shack. Some, mostly the men, were very businesslike. They marched up and down the rows until they found the right tree. Then they had it cut, paid for, and roped to the top of their car in no time flat.

The families with small children, and the young couples, always seemed to know how to make it fun. They wandered down the rows, discussing the good and bad things about each tree. The children rolled snowballs and made tiny snowmen among the pines while their parents debated. To these people, getting a tree never seemed like a chore. And these were the same families who always stopped in the sale shack for a cup of steaming hot chocolate or cider, and stayed to talk about Christmas as they sipped their drinks from Styrofoam cups. When they left with their trees, they always left behind a little Christmas spirit and the shack seemed a bit warmer for it. Shannon always liked helping these families the best.

Dad let her and Christa help pull the trees down the hill. Christa didn't mind the ropes like some horses would. She always stayed calm and waited for her mistress to tell her what to do next. Shannon didn't know if it was the warm Christmas spirit that filled her during these times, or the fact that she loved her pony so much, but somehow it never seemed like work.

After pulling several trees down the hill, Shannon stood next to Christa, leaned into her neck, and kissed the mare. *Why can't Amanda see how harmless Christa is?* Shannon wondered. Out of the corner of her eye she caught Amanda watching her, and she smiled.

By noon, the snow had really set in. It was as if the heavens had opened up, dumping tons of angel-like flakes on Christmas Tree Farm. Road crews began plowing and salting the roads, clearing the white stuff almost as fast as it came down. By then, the customers had stopped coming and Shannon and Amanda were free to do as they pleased.

Just outside the barn, Amanda lifted her face to the sky and stuck out her tongue to catch snowflakes.

Shannon brushed the snow from Christa's back and rubbed her dry with a cloth. Then she threw a big red saddle blanket over the pony's back. "Let's ride without a saddle today," she suggested. "We can pretend we're Susquehannock Indians. We can even find something in the hills to track in the snow!"

"Did the Susquehannocks ride horses?"

"I don't know." Shannon thought a moment. "But since we *are* pretending, it doesn't matter," she said.

Amanda shrugged. "Okay," she replied. "But I think we need a saddle. I'm afraid of falling off."

Shannon rolled her eyes. "Don't be such a scaredy-cat! Christa would NEVER dump us!"

"All right," Amanda gave in, "as long as you don't go fast. It feels funny when we don't have a saddle . . . more slippery."

"We'll just stay at a walk," Shannon promised. She slid from the fence onto Christa's back and then put out a hand to help tug Amanda aboard.

The snow continued to fall as the girls rode among the pine trees. They didn't talk, except in occasional whispers.

"Keep your eye out for something to track," Shannon murmured, and Amanda nodded.

A moment later, a rabbit darted out from under a pine tree. Leaping and bounding, he wove from tree to tree, leaving tracks in the fresh powder.

The moment the rabbit appeared, Christa's head and ears shot up. She snorted and sidestepped as the rabbit darted past, then put her head down and began to pursue the little creature. Shannon let the mare have her head. She had wanted something to track, and it seemed as if Christa knew that, so she just sat on the little horse and allowed her to follow the rabbit.

Amanda giggled and held tight to Shannon. "The way Christa is going after that bunny, she acts more like a dog than a pony."

Shannon laughed, too, as they reached another tree and Christa's big nose rooted the rabbit out from under it. They followed the rabbit up the hill, wandering from tree to tree, until at last it found shelter beneath some rocks that even Christa could not get her nose into. Christa stood with her nostrils glued to the rock for a moment. She pawed at the fresh snow, then finally gave up.

Shannon looked to see how far they had come. She was surprised to find that they were almost at Rattlesnake Hill. Motioning with her hand, she asked Amanda, "Do you want to go up and look around again?"

Amanda stared up the hill, through the gray haze of swirling flakes, until Shannon had to prod her for an answer. "Sure," she finally said. Shannon thought she heard a tremor in her friend's voice.

She nudged Christa with her heels, and they started up the hill. The air grew heavy and still. Only the whisper of swirling flakes could be heard, and the occasional echo of the wind dashing against the dark boulders. They rode until they were alongside the rocks. Then they wove between them until they came to the boulder where they had seen the carving of "Ahrwud and Frieda."

"Do you want to get off and look?" Shannon asked.

"No. Let's just look from here."

This time, Shannon knew there was fear in Amanda's voice, and under her warm snowsuit, she shivered, too. Something about this place was just plain eerie.

The boulders were all covered with snow. Shannon pulled Christa up close to the one that had had the carvings on it.

Reaching down, Amanda began to wipe the snow

away. Finally, she found the carving.

Shannon read it aloud. "Ahrwud and Frieda," it said, in those jagged letters.

Then Amanda brushed more snow away. "Look," she whispered.

Shannon leaned closer to the rock and scraped away more snow until she could see what Amanda had seen. Then she froze.

Under the names, a new word had been scratched in the same crooked way. "HELP!"

seven

T his isn't fun anymore," Shannon whispered.

Amanda was transfixed, staring at the rock in silence.

"Amanda!" Shannon elbowed her buddy. "Let's get out of here." She backed Christa out of the rocks and started down the hill.

Everything was still and quiet. It was as if every

branch waving overhead, every bush that huddled protectively around the rocks, was determined to keep the secret of Rattlesnake Hill. Not even the snow, falling all around them, seeing all, would breathe a sound or give up the secret. And all of it, the trees, the bushes, the snow, and the rocks had begun to seem cold and barren and downright scary.

They had only gone a few hundred feet when Amanda yelled out, "Stop!"

Shannon jerked back on the reins. "What?"

"In the snow! Look! Something blue."

Shannon looked. Then she saw what they had almost stepped on. A blue handle poked out of the snow between the mess of hoofprints and rabbit tracks they had made on their way up the hill. She slid from the horse, reached down, and pulled the blue thing out of the snow. It was a penknife.

After Shannon remounted, she handed the penknife to Amanda, who turned the flat, cylindrical piece over in her hand. She eyed the blue inlay and a grin lit up her face.

"What are you smiling at?"

"Proof!" Amanda said. Then, in answer to Shannon's questioning look, she continued. "This is Larry's penknife. I bet he dropped it here after scratching 'HELP' in the rock!"

"How do you know it's his?"

"Remember when Larry told me to cut the burlap? He handed me his knife and I got a good look at it. It was blue on the sides, just like this one."

"I can't believe he would do this!" Shannon's voice rose with bitterness. "At first it was funny," she admitted. "But he went too far!"

As they plodded down the hill slowly, in the face of falling snow, a large flock of black grackles rose from the gully, screeching and cawing angrily. Shannon jumped as the birds glided overhead.

"Something must be over there!"

"Maybe it's Larry watching us."

"Well, let him watch!" Shannon yelled. She felt the anger begin to boil inside. "We know it's you, Larry!" she hollered, but the hair still rose on her neck as the birds squawked and circled.

She nudged Christa to go faster and faster, until they were trotting down the hill. Shannon was hurt and scared and angry all rolled into one. She wanted to get away from Rattlesnake Hill and never come back again.

"Shannon!" Amanda yelled. "Stop! You're going down the hill too fast!"

Shannon bent her head low over the pony's back and urged her on. Pine trees passed by in a blur. She could feel Amanda's grip tighten on her waist.

"Shannon!" Amanda squealed.

Finally, Shannon pulled back on the reins, but at that very moment a rabbit leaped out from under a tree. Christa sidestepped suddenly, then stumbled. She went down on her knees, skidding through the snow until her hindquarters collapsed, too. Both girls went flying, and tumbled down the hill.

Shannon felt herself rolling, her sides scraping the cold snow, her legs and arms flailing wildly. She came to a stop on her back, staring up into the gray sky that was still releasing a thick haze of flakes. She reached up to brush them away and felt pain flash through her side when she moved. She could see Amanda rising to stand just a few yards farther down the hill, and Christa stumbling to her hooves. Amanda came over to Shannon slowly.

"Are you all right?" Shannon asked.

She noticed Amanda's chin was quivering and tears streaked her face. "I'm fine. How about you?"

"I don't know. My side hurts," Shannon said. She pushed herself up to a sitting position, then tried to stand. A sudden, wincing pain shot through her ankle and she collapsed again. "I can't stand," she said. She felt anger and other emotions swirling inside her. Some she didn't even recognize. She was scared. She knew that. And her ankle hurt—bad.

Christa ambled over to the girls. She shoved her warm nostrils against Shannon, as if to check on her mistress.

All at once, Amanda jumped as a dark blur came toward the girls. She spun around. Someone bundled in a heavy coat and a baseball cap was hurrying toward them.

"Are you girls okay?" he called out.

Shannon let out the breath she was holding. It was only Larry. Awful, sweet, ornery Larry. She had wanted to smack him and yell at him for all the tricks, but just now, she was glad to see him.

"I'm okay," Amanda told him. "But Shannon's hurt. She can't walk."

Larry dropped to his knees in front of Shannon. He rolled up her snow pants to look at the leg she was holding and stared down at the ankle. Already it was swollen and turning purple. He felt for bumps as Shannon held her breath. Then Larry rolled down the pant leg again. An anxious look filled his face.

"Do you hurt anywhere else?" he asked.

"Yes. My ribs hurt, right here." She touched the spot gently, then pulled her hand away.

Larry looked at Amanda. "If it were just the ankle we could let her ride . . ." Larry hesitated. "But her side hurts, too. We can't take a chance on moving her," he said. "You're going to have to go for help, while I stay here and keep her warm."

Even as he spoke, Larry was removing his heavy coat and slipping it under Shannon, wrapping the big sides up and around her. "Take Christa," he added.

Amanda's mouth dropped open. "I . . . I can't!" she stammered. "I don't know how to ride alone. I . . . I'm afraid!"

"You have to," Larry said firmly. "Shannon needs help. All you have to do is give that pony her head. She's as gentle as a lamb and I know she'll head for home. Don't you worry."

Larry stood up and reached for Christa's reins. "I'll give you a leg up."

"But what if she runs? What if I fall off?"

Larry patted Amanda's shoulder. "She won't run unless you squeeze or kick her sides. That's her signal to hurry up. Just let her head for home. If she wanders, take the reins, and guide her back on course. You've seen Shannon do it enough."

Amanda started to protest, then she looked down

at Shannon's face. Her eyes were closed and she was breathing as if she was in pain. "Okay," she said.

Larry boosted Amanda onto Christa's back. Shannon opened her eyes. "You'll be fine," she said. "You can count on Christa. She can do almost anything."

Shannon snuggled deeper into the warm lining of Larry's coat and watched as Christa started down the hill. Amanda took the reins in her hands and sat up tall.

As her two best friends headed down the hill, Shannon shivered. Her ankle was throbbing now, and her side burned. Amanda had to make it home and return with help before it was too dark to see.

eight

Shannon let out her breath slowly as Christa disappeared into the falling flakes. Amanda's back had been straight and rigid, but the reins were in her hands and she was heading in the right direction. Shannon crossed her fingers and mumbled a quick prayer. The sky was the same shade of gray it had been since the snow began, but she knew it must be getting close to suppertime. Her stomach rumbled with hunger.

Shannon watched as Larry walked part way down the hill, watching Amanda for as long as he could. Now, as he walked toward Shannon, the mix of emotions began to swirl inside of her again. This was all his fault! If he hadn't started the whole mess with his silly stories . . . Shannon took a deep breath. As Larry knelt beside her and the thickness of silence and snow settled in, she decided she had to know the truth.

Pushing herself up on one elbow, she stared at Larry. He had pulled his cap down over his eyes to ward off the wind and snow and she couldn't see his face.

"There are no ghosts, are there?" She said it plainly, matter-of-factly.

"What?"

"There are no ghosts!" Shannon felt the mix of emotions rise to the surface and spill over. "There's no mine, no Ahrwud, no Frieda, no silver, no truth!"

Larry turned to stare at Shannon. He seemed

startled by the outburst.

"You wanted us to chase your legend, didn't you? You carved things in the rock just to make us think it was real! You followed us when we came up here. You tried to scare us! Didn't you, Larry?"

Larry rubbed his hands together. Shannon didn't know if he was getting cold or if it was his guilt making him nervous. Either way, she didn't care. She just wanted an answer.

"I don't know if the legend is true. I don't know if the ghosts are real," he answered. "The legend has been around a lot longer than I have and a lot of people, grown-up people, think it *is* true." Larry reached up and rubbed his brow under the bill of his cap. "But you're right," he admitted. "I did carve the things in the rocks. I did follow you. I didn't want to scare you. I swear it. I only wanted to give you an adventure."

"But you did scare us," Shannon accused. "Why did you do that?"

"When I was a kid, growing up on the other side

of Rattlesnake Hill, I searched for the mine, too. I wanted to find the silver so bad that I would dream about Ahrwud and Frieda. I guess some small part of me still believes that a silver mine is up here." He swept his hand up toward the hill. "Some part of me believes there is silver waiting to be found. When you and Amanda decided to go search, I started to hope again. Maybe two girls *could* find what all those grown-ups missed."

"That would have been fine," Shannon said. Her voice had softened. "But then you went and tricked us with all those clues. You heard us talking, too. You knew we thought someone was watching and that we were afraid. Why didn't you tell us it was only you?"

Larry rubbed his hands again, and then his arms. "I wasn't planning to scratch anything into the rock. That first day I was up here poking around and I saw the two of you coming. All at once, I just thought it would be funny to leave a clue. I scratched 'Ahrwud and Frieda' into the rock, brushed away my tracks with a pine branch, and hid. You two were so excited when you saw those names! I remembered being that excited as a kid."

Shannon saw the guilt in Larry's eyes and her anger melted.

"I saw you two heading out again today and decided to do it again. It was easy to get ahead of you. The way you two were chasing after that rabbit, you didn't even see me passing by just two rows of trees over. I guess I got caught up in the fun of it and didn't think about your feelings."

Shannon rubbed Larry's arm. He wasn't such a bad guy.

"I'm sorry," Larry said gently.

Shannon was about to say it was okay, that she understood, when she realized the material under her fingertips was thin. Larry only had a flannel shirt on! No wonder he had been rubbing his hands and arms so much. He was freezing! She had forgotten that Larry had wrapped his coat around her.

"Larry." She touched his arm. "You should get under this coat with me before you freeze!"

"You mean you forgive me?"

"Yes." Shannon pulled the heavy fur-lined suede up and over his arms as he slid in beside her. "But don't go trying to trick us again!" she warned in a half-serious voice. "I might not be so easy on you next time!"

Ducking under the coat they breathed heavily, trying to ward off the cold flakes and fill the tented coat with warm air. It was quiet again, but it wasn't an uncomfortable silence this time.

"How long have they been gone?" she whispered.

Larry checked his watch. "About forty-five minutes. Help should be along anytime now."

Shannon peeked out at the gray, snow-filled sky. It seemed a shade darker. "Do you think they'll make it before night?"

Larry gazed out from under the coat. "I think . . ." He hesitated, then sat upright, peering into the white snow. "I think I can safely say yes to that question," he said, grinning broadly, "because here they come now!"

Shannon followed Larry's gaze, then she saw them, too. Amanda was leading a small group up the hill, and amazingly, she was still riding Christa! Behind her was Shannon's dad and several men in paramedic uniforms.

Larry stood up and waved. "We're up here," he called.

Shannon scooted into a stiff upright position. Pain shot through her side, but she smiled just the same, at Larry and her dad, at the paramedics, and especially at Amanda, who sat astride Christa with the most satisfied smile Shannon had ever seen.

nine

Amanda arrived just after dinner on Christmas. Dad hooked Christa up to the sleigh and Shannon and Amanda met him outside for a moonlit sleigh ride.

Dad helped Shannon into the back of the sleigh, propping her sprained ankle up on the edge. She was lucky that a sprained ankle and a scrape on her side were all she had suffered in her fall on Rattlesnake Hill.

After they had climbed into the back of the sleigh, Shannon and Amanda exchanged two tiny boxes.

"Merry Christmas!" Amanda said. "I hope you like it."

"Open yours first," Shannon insisted.

Amanda unwrapped the box and peered inside. Then she sucked in her breath and lifted a beautiful silver-colored brooch from the tissue. "Is it really for me?"

"Yes! Isn't it neat?" Shannon pointed to an identical pin on her own sweater. "Mom had them made for us, so we could remember our adventure. They're just like Great-Grandmother Schmitt's brooch that you found, except yours has your initials and mine has my initials!"

Amanda hugged Shannon, then pinned the brooch to her blouse. "This is the best gift ever! Open yours!"

Shannon slid the paper from her box and lifted

the lid. Two earrings shaped like golden saddles gleamed beneath the tissue paper.

"That's so you remember that I like to ride with a saddle!" Amanda kidded.

Shannon laughed as she clipped an earring to each ear. "The neat thing is that now you *do* like to ride!" she said. She looked thoughtful. "We'll never forget this winter, will we?" she added.

"Nope! We'll remember it forever!" Amanda agreed.

The moon shone in the sky like a giant silver Christmas ball. A sprinkling of stars surrounded the ball like sparkling Christmas lights. Dad clicked to Christa and the sleigh slid across the freshly powdered road as smooth as a skater on a glassy pond. As the trees glided by and the snowy banks beside the road shone white and looming, Shannon and Amanda huddled close in the back of the sleigh, warm under the big woolen blanket Mom had provided.

"This was the best adventure ever," Shannon whispered.

"Yes," Amanda agreed. "Perfect."

Christa's hooves clicked across the frozen ground and Shannon thought about all that had happened. It's funny, she thought, how things turn out. Amanda had finally overcome her fear of riding alone, even though she had taken a spill from Christa on Rattlesnake Hill. Larry had promised to cut back on the tricks he played. But the lost silver mine of Rattlesnake Hill had still not been found.

Shannon realized that every single thing that happened had happened because of another person, not a ghost. None of it was exceptional, except for the finding of Great-Grandmother Schmitt's old silver brooch. Maybe it was silly to have tried to find the silver mine or to even believe a ghost could exist.

Rubbing the brooch that was pinned to her coat, she realized that Mom's favorite saying was true. Every cloud did have a silver lining. For her, the adventure had been worth the scary parts. She closed her eyes and pictured the rocks on Rattlesnake Hill, wondering if the Hill, like a cloud, still had a silver lining.

Staring up at Rattlesnake Hill, Shannon saw a million stars shining in the sky above.

"It was silly for us to believe in ghosts," she said out loud.

"Yes," Amanda agreed. Then she grabbed Shannon's mittened hand in her own and they both turned to gaze up at the place where they had found adventure.

All at once, a blaze of white lit up the sky. A falling star streaked across the purple heavens, right over Rattlesnake Hill. Without a thought, Shannon closed her eyes and made a wish. She crossed her fingers to cement the wish, then turned to look at Amanda. Amanda had seen the star, too. Her fingers were crossed and her eyes were closed.

"What did you wish for?" Shannon whispered.

"Another chance to find the lost silver mine," Amanda whispered back.

"That's what I wished for, too," Shannon said.

The moon slid out from behind the clouds, lighting up Rattlesnake Hill and casting two ghostly white shadows over the rocks above. Shannon huddled closer to Amanda and grinned. "Ahrwud and Frieda . . ." she whispered, and Amanda nodded.

Check out these other enchanting *Charming Ponies* books!

A Perfect Pony

It's the most exciting day of Niki's life! She's saved up enough money to buy her very own pony, and today is the day of the pony auction. She could take home a magnificent pinto or a proud thoroughbred, but she sets her heart on a beautiful white mare instead. When a little black horse with big sad eyes distracts Niki from the mare of her dreams, will she miss the chance to own the perfect pony?

A Pony Promise

Tiffany Clark has to keep her big brother's family secret, and it's not easy. Luckily she can confide in Windy, the pinto mare at Mr. Paul's horse farm. But when Windy and a mare named Stormy give birth within days of each other, there's a problem. It's going to take a miracle for Stormy's foal to survive, and nothing short of a horse adoption can save the day. Will Windy agree to raise another mare's foal?

HarperFestival
A Division of HarperCollinsPublishers

www.harpercollinschildrens.com